With special thanks to the James R. Thorpe Foundation who made this book and other resources possible through a grant to the Minnesota Coalition For Terminal Care for Project S.S.A.D. (Someone Special And Death)

ISBN-13: 978-0-9620502-0-6
ISBN-10: 0-9620502-0-2

WOODLAND PRESS
8104 Highwood Drive, #G-226
Bloomington, MN 55438
(952) 830-9423

PRINTED IN THE U.S.A.

ADDITIONAL COPIES: For individual copies send $9.95 plus applicable tax and $3.00 to cover the cost of handling to WOODLAND PRESS.
QUANTITY DISCOUNT RATES are available for hospitals, schools, churches and others who need more than 12 copies. Write for details.

A FACILITATOR GUIDE is available for $30.00 and includes additional information for leading a structured children's grief support group.
FACILITATOR TRAINING WORKSHOPS are offered in Minneapolis, MN. Contact Woodland Press for more information.

This book is written for grieving children and is dedicated to my three sons who were 9, 10 and 12 when their father died.

HOW ADULTS CAN HELP CHILDREN COPE WITH DEATH AND GRIEF

It is often helpful for adults to seek additional support and education to understand their own grief process and model a healthy reaction to loss by expressing their feelings and receiving support. Children will generally learn their response to loss from adults in the family.

Children may feel frightened and insecure because they sense the grief and stress of others, and feel powerless to help. They will need additional love, support and structure in their daily routine.

When someone dies, children often worry about themselves and others dying. They need to know who would take care of them in the unlikely death of both parents.

They need an adequate explanation of the cause of death, using correct terms like die and dead. Vague terms and trying to shield them from the truth merely adds confusion. Avoid terms that associate going away, sleep, or sickness with death. Listen carefully to a child's response.

Children have magical thinking and may believe that their behavior or thoughts can cause or reverse death.

Do not exclude children when family or friends come to comfort grieving adults. Avoidance or silence teaches children that death is a taboo subject. Children need to learn how to cope with loss, not be protected from grief.

Help children learn to recognize, name, accept and express feelings to avoid developing unhealthy defenses to cope with difficult emotions. Make physical and creative activities available for energy outlets.

A child may try to protect grieving adults and try to assume the caretaker role, but children need to grow up normally without being burdened with adult responsibilities.

Help children learn to cope with other losses. The death of a pet is a very significant loss for a child. The patterns for coping with loss and grief begin in early childhood and often continue through adulthood.

Share personal religious beliefs carefully. Children may fear or resent a God that takes to heaven someone they love and need.

A child's grief may not be recognized because children express feelings of grief more in behavior than in words. Feelings of abandonment, helplessness, despair, anxiety, apathy, anger, guilt and fear are common and often acted out aggressively because children may be unable to express feelings verbally.

ABOUT THIS BOOK

This is a book designed for children, ages 6-12, to illustrate with pictures they choose to draw. Do not make suggestions. They need very few directions or distractions as they use symbols, lines and colors to tell their personal story. It is important that a parent or caring adult be available to read the concepts of each unit, and accept their non-verbal expressions without probing deeply. It is all right to ask them if they can tell you more about a picture to encourage communication.

Focus on their ideas and expressions instead of their drawing ability. This book is intended to be their true story, not a pretty picture book. Listen carefully and be aware that words, adults use, may have several meanings that confuse children. If pictures reveal misconceptions, be gentle with any corrections, recognizing that what a child thinks can be as powerful as what actually happened.

This book was designed to be used just once weekly for $1-1^1/_2$ hours, but individual needs may vary. The educational concepts are divided into 6 units with specific objectives for each unit. Additional reading is suggested to stress concepts further, and several books are listed in each unit.

Children need to know that this is a book to help them learn about death and the feelings of grief. It cannot be done quickly. It takes time, but it is something they will be able to keep to help them remember someone very special.

Each child will need a basic box of 8 crayons to illustrate their story. Crayons are suggested because they are more effective for expressing various feelings than markers that flow freely, regardless of pressure. Children like to illustrate their books because they naturally think in terms of symbols, instead of words, until sometime between the ages of 9 and 12. Older children may prefer colored pencils and use more words.

Adults may want to work on their own journal or book at this time, recording their own personal feelings, thoughts and memories to share. Children learn to mourn by observing adults. Do not try to protect children from difficult feelings. Help them to understand and express feelings so they will be able to develop coping skills for the natural difficulties of life.

This book was designed to teach children death education, to recognize and express feelings of grief, encourage open communication, and help adults discover unhealthy misconceptions the child may have. The concepts needed to teach the following objectives are included in the following text, but may be stressed further by additional reading suggested.

I. CHANGE IS PART OF LIFE p.1-6
    See change as a natural part of growth
    Discuss personal change/losses
    Identify ways of coping with change
    Discuss changes related to death

ADDITIONAL READING
    The Very Hungry Caterpillar, E. Carle
    Life Times, Mellonie and Ingpen
    Who Will Wake Up Spring? S. Lerner

II. DEAD IS THE END OF LIVING p.7-11
    Learn basic concepts of death education
    Assess understanding of cause of death
    Identify personal misconceptions
    Accept reality of loss

ADDITIONAL READING
    A Look At Death, M. Forrai
    Talking About Death, E. Grollman
    About Dying, S.B. Stein

III. LIVING MEANS FEELING p.12-18
    Learn that all kinds of feelings are o.k.
    Begin to recognize/name basic feelings
    Encourage acceptance/sharing of feelings
    Identify ways to express negative feelings

ADDITIONAL READING
    Feelings, Alika
    I Was So Mad! M. Mayer
    The Colors That I Am, C. Shehan

IV. FEELING BETTER p. 19-22
    Identify fears and worries
    Recognize individual strengths
    Increase confidence and self esteem
    Learn ways to communicate concerns

ADDITIONAL READING
    What Makes Me Feel This Way? E. LeShan
    I Have Feelings, Terry Berger
    Someone Special Died, J. Prestine

V. SHARING MEMORIES p.23-27
    Discuss painful memories
    Identify feelings of being responsible
    Recognize losses
    Reinforce positive memories

ADDITIONAL READING
    Why Did Grampa Die? B. Hazen
    When My Dad Died, J. Hammond
    Stories From Snowy Meadow, C. Steven

VI. I'M SPECIAL TOO p.28-32
    Identify support systems
    Describe basic concepts of relationships
    Celebrate completion of book
    Share memories and feelings with family

ADDITIONAL READINGS
    Man About The House, J. Fassler
    Sometimes I'm Afraid, J. Fassler
    A Taste Of Blackberries, D. Smith

TO GRIEVING CHILDREN:

This is a book written to help you through a difficult time. When someone you love dies, no one can take the loss and pain away. Yet, it does help to learn some facts about death and the feelings of grief, and I hope you will learn it is o.k. to talk about these things.

This is not intended to be a book of beautiful pictures. You do not have to be able to draw or color well. You can use colors, lines and shapes and a few words to make pictures that will tell your own personal story.

Do the first four pictures and then take some time to think and talk with someone about what you did before you do the next four.

You will want to keep this book in a safe place to read again when you get older, and more able to understand this confusing time.

change is natural. Draw or color some ↓

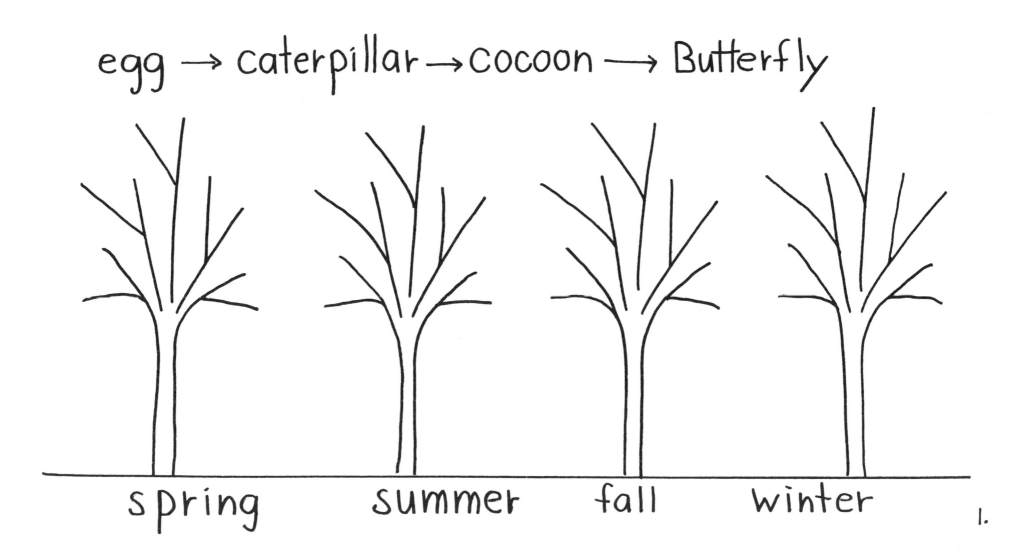

egg → caterpillar → cocoon → Butterfly

spring   summer   fall   winter

People Change too

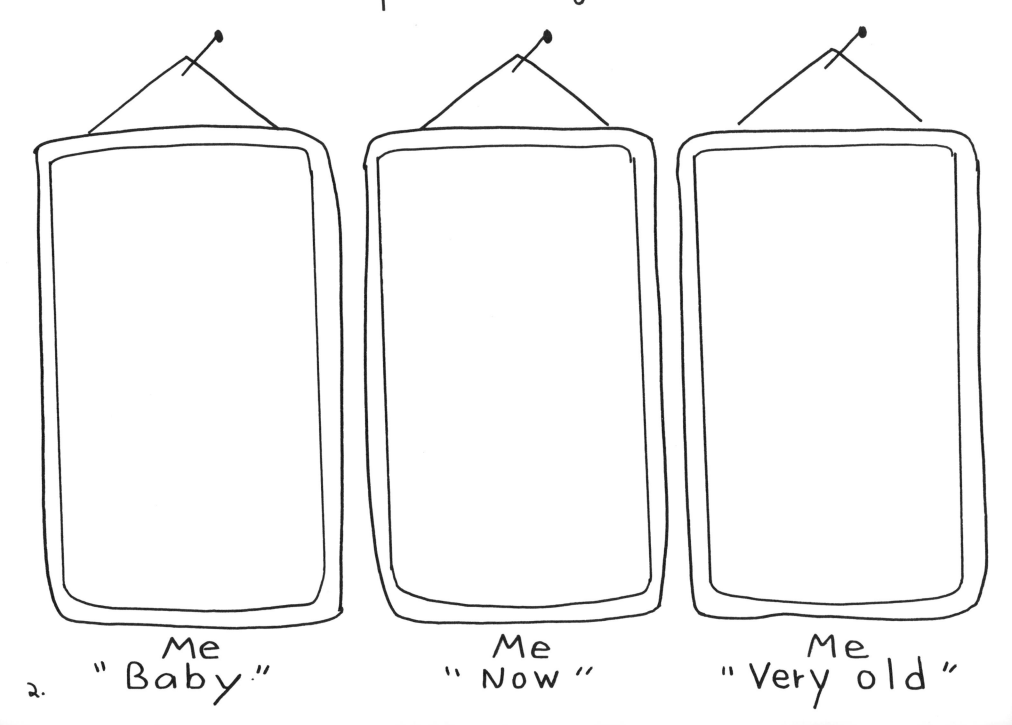

Me "Baby"

Me "Now"

Me "Very old"

2.

Change creates loss
The pain from loss is called grief

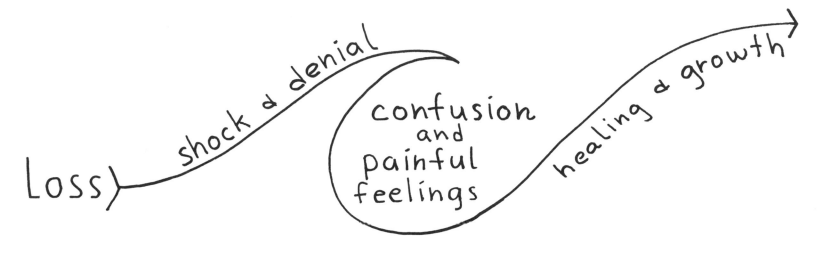

Loss)

shock & denial

confusion and painful feelings

healing & growth

Grief comes and goes
Like waves in the ocean

There will be <u>stormy</u> times and <u>calm</u> times !

Living is growing and changing. Dead is the end of living. Plants die... Animals die... People die...

Living

dead

Death is a <u>natural</u> part of living

4.

Many different things cause people
to die. (Draw some things that cause death)

But people can't die because of anything
we <u>think</u> or <u>say</u> !!

5.

Someone I loved died. This is a
picture of that person...

_____ was
(name)

important to me
because...

6.

My Special Person died because...

when someone dies, they can never come
back! Death is the end of living. The dead
don't eat, sleep, think, or feel anything. 7.

People have a body we can see... and something called a spirit or soul which we cannot see that makes them special.

When someone dies, the spirit leaves the body, and what is left is placed in a casket to be buried or cremated.

8.

Family and friends gather for a <u>funeral service</u> to honor the dead, remember the good they did, and show their love for you!

It's hard to say <u>goodbye</u> to someone you love!

9.

Some people think the spirit goes to heaven to be with God, and some think it takes a new form... like the caterpillar that becomes a butterfly. Others think the spirit becomes a part of those they loved. (draw what you think)

We don't know everything about death!

10.

There are things I <u>wonder</u> about.
I would like to ask someone these
questions...

Everyone has lots of different feelings.
They are all OK! Feelings change.

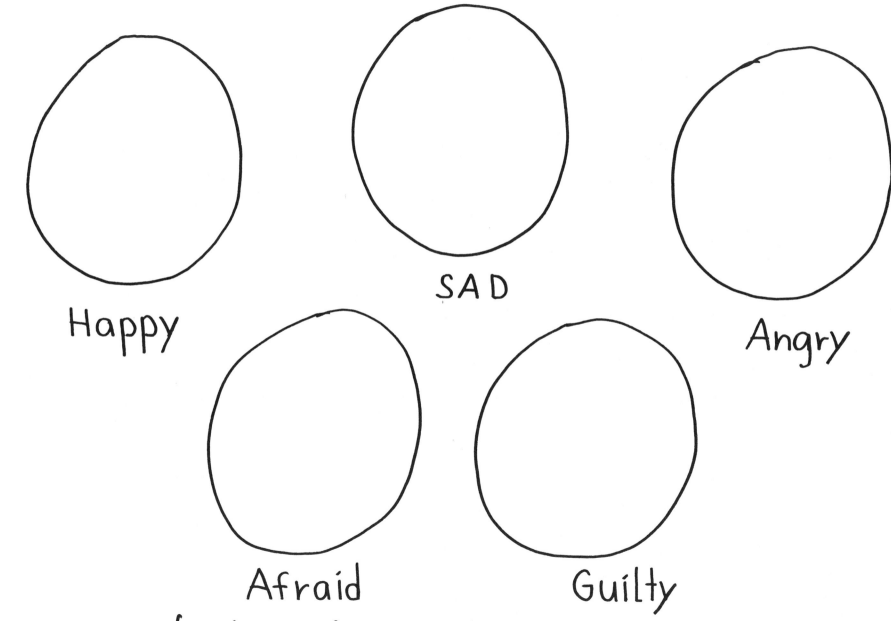

Happy

SAD

Angry

Afraid

Guilty

Draw some feeling faces...(feelings often show on faces)

12.

Sometimes people put on a "mask" to hide feelings they don't like to show. (name and draw 3 feelings you sometimes hide with a different feeling.)

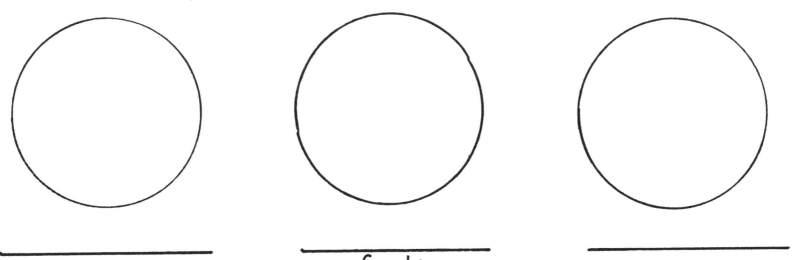

Name and draw the feeling masks you might use.

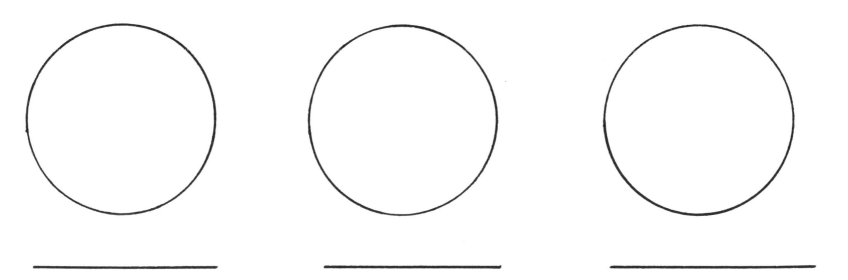

Feelings are something we <u>feel in our body</u>.

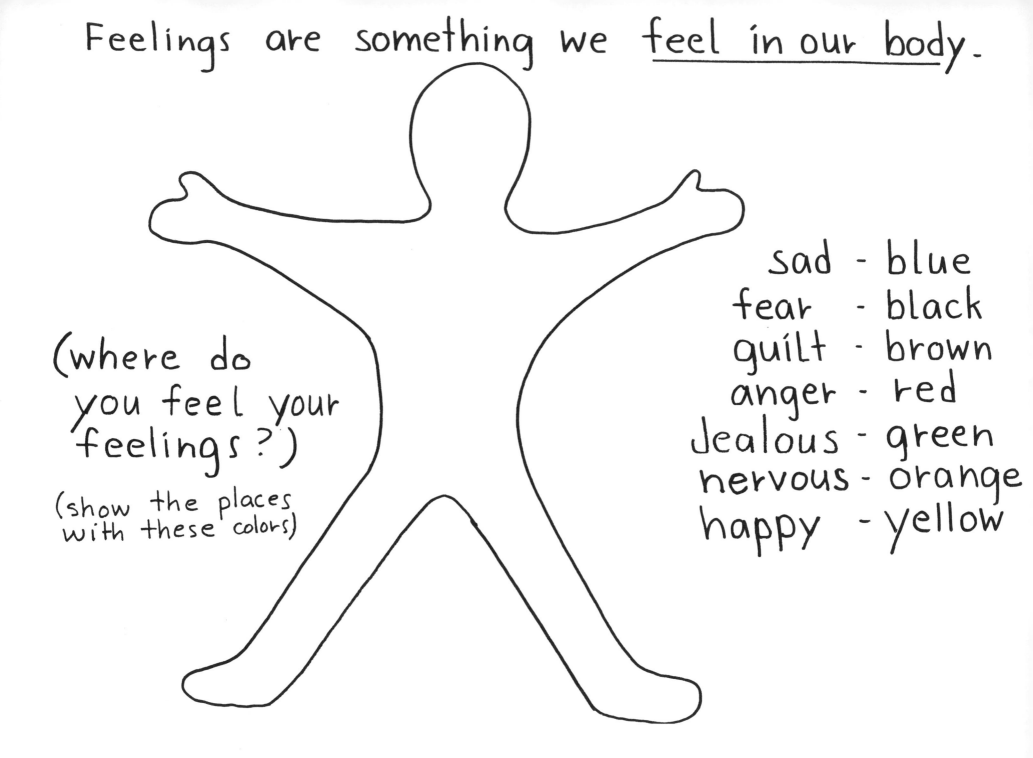

(where do you feel your feelings?)

(show the places with these colors)

sad - blue
fear - black
guilt - brown
anger - red
Jealous - green
nervous - orange
happy - yellow

14.

If feelings are stuffed inside <u>too long</u> they often cause <u>aches</u> and <u>pains</u>

color red <u>lightly</u> where you get <u>little</u> hurts.

color <u>bright</u> red where you sometimes hurt <u>alot</u>!

Is this the <u>same</u> place you keep <u>fear</u> or <u>anger</u> or other feelings?

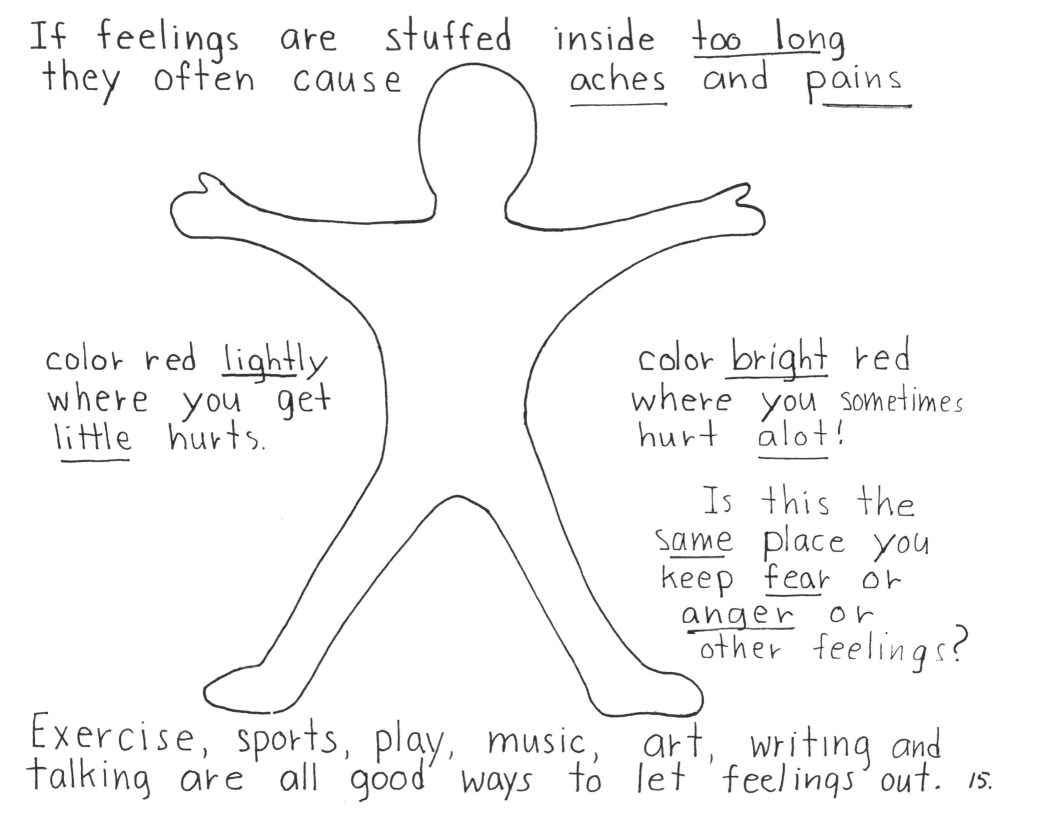

Exercise, sports, play, music, art, writing and talking are all good ways to let feelings out. 15.

Something Sad

16. Drawing out sadness takes some of the pain away.

Sometimes I get angry because...

Putting anger on paper doesn't hurt anyone!

It is important to let anger out in ways that will <u>not</u> <u>hurt</u> <u>people</u> or <u>things</u>. O.K. ways are:

1. Saying "I am angry because..."
2. Scribbling with a red crayon on an old newspaper (hard!) and scrunch it into a ball to throw away.
3. Punching a ball or a pillow.
4. Yelling into a pillow or in a shower.
5. Writing an angry letter. Tear it up.
6. Write feelings in a journal.
7. Run or walk fast.
8. Stomp your feet. Clap your hands.

I feel frightened when...

Drawing something fearful makes it less powerful.

19.

I worry about...

20. Worries need to be <u>shared</u> with someone!

Sometimes I feel <u>different</u> because...

But these are things I <u>like</u> <u>about</u> <u>me</u>...

    1.

    2.

    3.

Me... doing something I am good at !

Everyone is good at something. No one is
22. good at every thing.

I remember being told about the death.

I needed love and comfort. I still do!

23.

I know how I like to be comforted...
(draw this... and then close your eyes and imagine it.)

24. I can use words to let others know what I need.

" If ONLY "

Everyone has something they wish they <u>did</u>...
or <u>didn't</u> do.

25.

My favorite memory

and other good memories are mine to keep !

26.

I learned something important from this person

and I will always have the love given to me! 27.

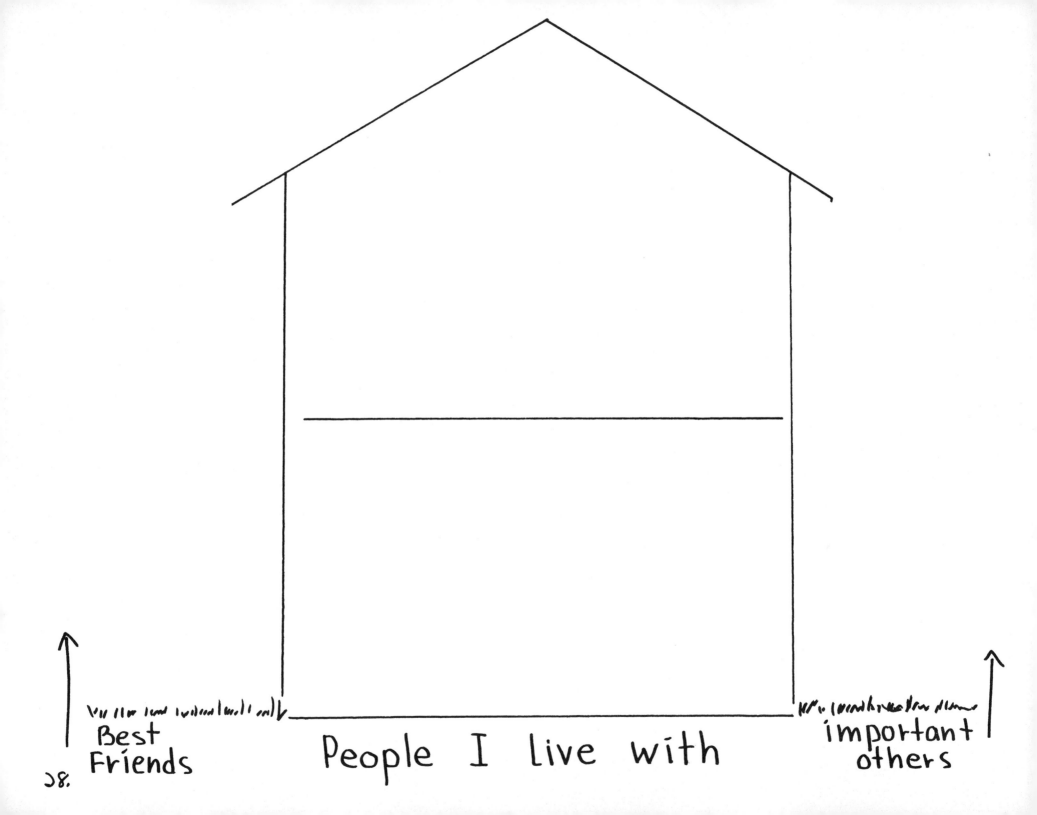

Best
Friends

⊃8.

People I live with

important
others

Many People care about me

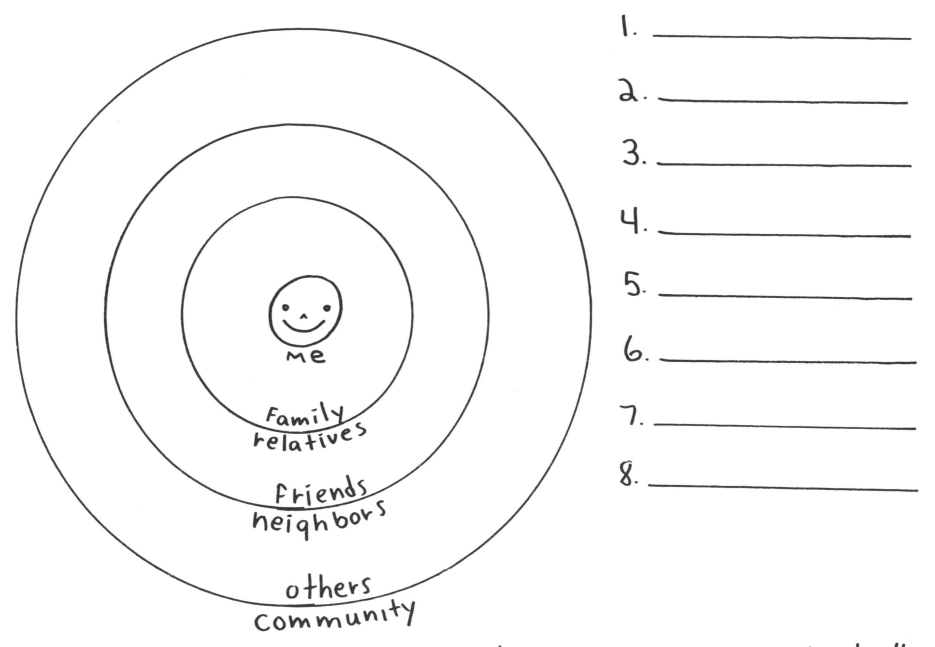

1. _____
2. _____
3. _____
4. _____
5. _____
6. _____
7. _____
8. _____

List names and place numbers in "caring circle".

I have someone I can always talk to.
(this can be a pet, a person or something special)

30.

I show others I care about them...

And that makes me special too!

31.

I can still have fun and be happy !

Living means changing and growing.

32.

The Drawing Out Feelings Series

This new series designed by Marge Heegaard provides parents and professionals with an organized approach to helping children ages 6-12 cope with feelings resulting from family loss and change.

Designed to be used in an adult/child setting, these workbooks provide age-appropriate educational concepts and questions to help children identify and accept their feelings. Children are given the opportunity to work out their emotions during difficult times while learning to recognize acceptable behavior, and conflicts can be resolved and self-esteem increased while the coping skills for loss and change are being developed.

All four titles are formatted so that children can easily illustrate their answers to the important questions in the text.

When Something Terrible Happens

A workbook to help children deal with their feelings about traumatic events.

Empowers children to explore feelings, and reduces nightmares and post-traumatic stress symptoms. "This healing book...combines story, pictures, information, and art therapy in a way that appeals to children." —Stephanie Frogge, Director of Victim Outreach, M.A.D.D.

Ages 6–12, 36 pp, 11x8 1/2"
trade paperback, ISBN 0-9620502-3-7 $9.95

When Mom and Dad Separate

A workbook to help children deal with their feelings about separation/divorce.

This bestselling workbook helps youngsters discuss the basic concepts of marriage and divorce, allowing them to work through all the powerful and confusing feelings resulting from their parents' decision to separate.

Ages 6-12, 36 pp, 11x8 1/2"
trade paperback, ISBN 0-9620502-2-9 $9.95

When Someone Has a Very Serious Illness

A workbook to help children deal with their feelings about serious illness.

An excellent resource for helping children learn the basic concepts of illness and various age-appropriate ways of coping with someone else's illness. "...offers children a positive tool for coping with those many changes." —Christine Ternand, M.D., Pediatrician

Ages 6–12, 41 pp, 11 x 8 1/2"
trade paperback, ISBN 0-9620502-4-5 $9.95

When Someone Very Special Dies
Children Can Learn to Cope with Grief

A workbook to help children deal with their feelings about death.

Here is a practical format for allowing children to understand the concept of death and develop coping skills for life. Children, with adult supervision, are invited to illustrate and personalize their loss through art. This workbook encourages the child to identify support systems and personal strengths. "I especially appreciate the design of this book...the child becomes an active participant in pictorially and verbally doing something about [their loss]." —Dean J. Hempel, M.D., Child Psychiatrist

Ages 6–12
36 pp, 11 x 8 1/2"
trade paperback
ISBN 0-9620502-0-2 $9.95

When a Family Is In Trouble
Children Can Cope With Grief From Drug and Alcohol Addictions

A workbook to help children through the trauma of a parent's chemical dependency problem.

This helpful workbook provides basic information about addictions and encourages healthy coping skills. Children express personal trauma and feelings more easily in pictures than in words, and the pages of this title are perfect to "draw out" those feelings and hurts. There is plenty of room for a child's artwork.

Ages 6–12
36 pp, 11 x 8 1/2"
trade paperback
ISBN 0-9620502-7-X $9.95

When a Parent Marries Again

A workbook to help children deal with their feelings about stepfamilies.

This book helps kids sort through unrealistic expectations, different values, divided loyalties, and family histories. It helps reduce the fear and stress surrounding remarriage and promotes greater family unity.

Ages 6–12, 36 pp, 11 x 8 1/2"
trade paperback, ISBN 0-9620502-6-1 $9.95

Facilitator Guide For DRAWING OUT FEELINGS

for
When Someone Very Special Dies
When Something Terrible Happens
When Someone Has a Very Serious Illness
When Mom and Dad Separate

Structure and suggestions for helping children, individually or in groups, cope with feelings from family change. Includes directions for six organized sessions for each of the four workbooks.
99 pp. 8x11 ISBN 0-9620502-5-3

$30.00

For Adults

Grief - *A Natural Reaction to Loss*

$9.95 PBK

6 X 9 • 96 PAGES